Draw It

Dona Herweck Rice

Library of Congress Cataloging-in-Publication Data

Names: Rice, Dona, author.
Title: Draw it / Dona Herweck Rice.
Description: Huntington Beach, CA : Teacher Created Materials, 2018. | Audience: Ages 4-6. |
Identifiers: LCCN 2018020225 (print) | LCCN 2018020703 (ebook) | ISBN 9781493898930 | ISBN 9781493898190 (pbk.)
Subjects: LCSH: Drawing--Technique--Juvenile literature.
Classification: LCC NC655 (ebook) | LCC NC655 .R525 2018 (print) | DDC 741.2--dc23
LC record available at https://lccn.loc.gov/2018020225

Publishing Credits

Rachelle Cracchiolo, M.S.Ed., *Publisher*
Conni Medina, M.A.Ed., *Managing Editor*
Nika Fabienke, Ed.D., *Content Director*
Véronique Bos, *Creative Director*
Shaun N. Bernadou, *Art Director*
Carol Huey-Gatewood, M.A.Ed., *Editor*
Valerie Morales, *Associate Editor*
Courtney Roberson, *Senior Graphic Designer*

Image Credits: All images from iStock and/or Shutterstock.

Teacher Created Materials
5301 Oceanus Drive
Huntington Beach, CA 92649-1030
www.tcmpub.com

ISBN 978-1-4938-9819-0

Printed by: 51497
Printed in: China

He  his  .

draws cat

He  draws his  dog.

He  his  .

draws house

He  his  .

draws car

He  his .

draws bear

He  his  .

draws kite

He  his .

draws cookie

He  his  .

draws apple

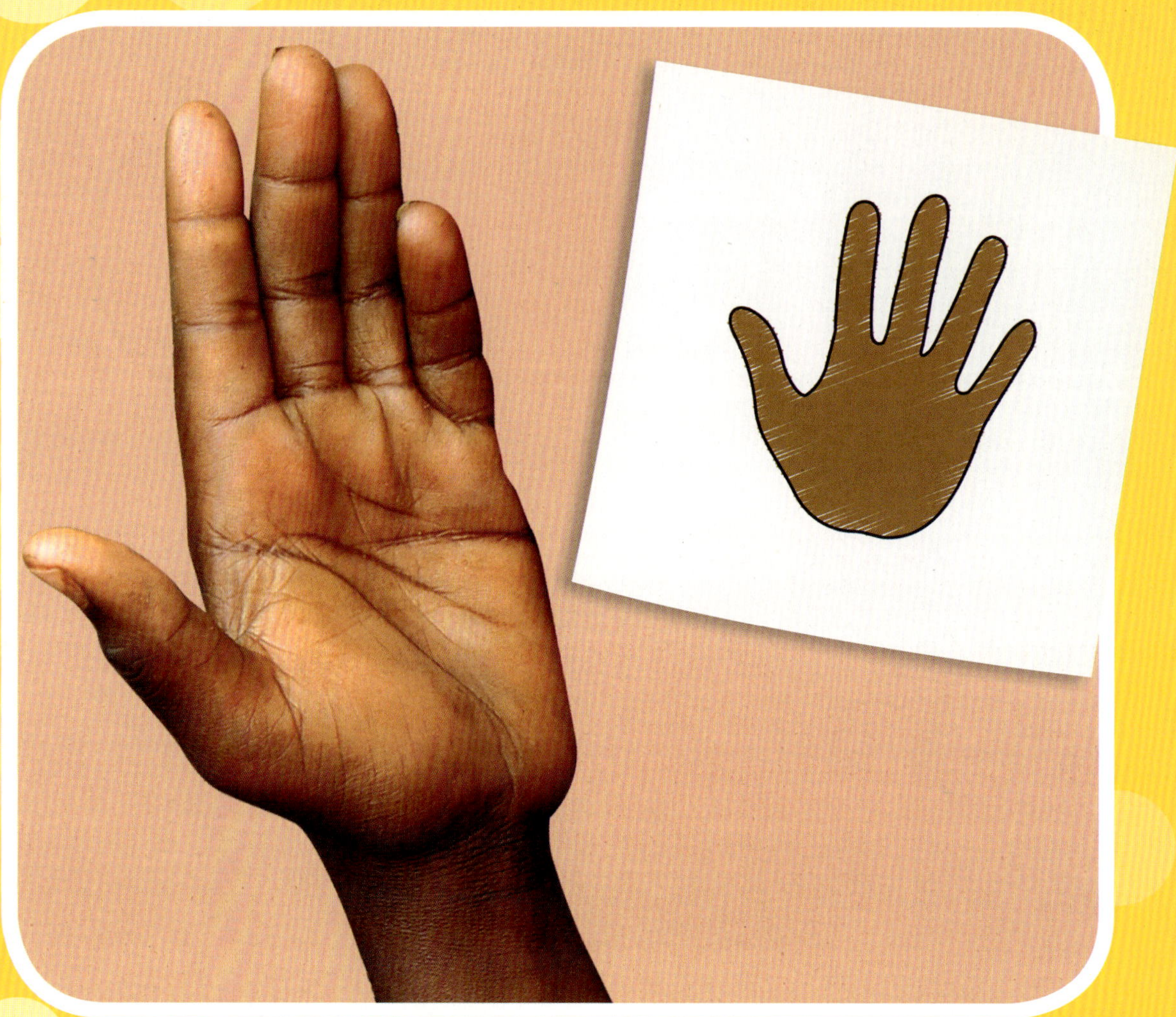

He  his 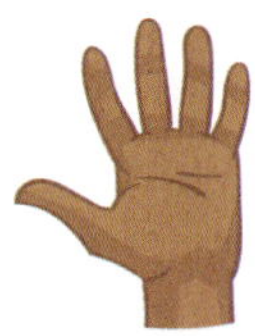 .

draws hand

He  his .

draws face

High-Frequency Words

he
his